Written by David Bedford
Illustrated by Brenna Vaughan and Henry St. Leger

First published 2013 by Parragon Books, Ltd.
Copyright © 2018 Cottage Door Press, LLC
5005 Newport Drive, Rolling Meadows, Illinois 60008
All Rights Reserved

10 9 8 7 6 5 4 3 2 1

ISBN 978-1-68052-542-7

Parragon Books is an imprint of Cottage Door Press, LLC.
Parragon Books® and the Parragon® logo are
registered trademarks of Cottage Door Press, LLC.

I love my Mommy

PaRragon.

One morning, Little Deer didn't want to
play around his home anymore.
"I want to see new things,"
he told his mommy.
"Then let's go exploring," said Mommy Deer,
"and see what new things we can find."

"This way!" said Little Deer excitedly,
and he hurried ahead, while Mommy followed
behind, watching over him.

Little Deer **hopped** along the grass by the hanging
willow tree. Then he slowly crossed the wobbly stones,
watching the stream as it trickled gently beside him.

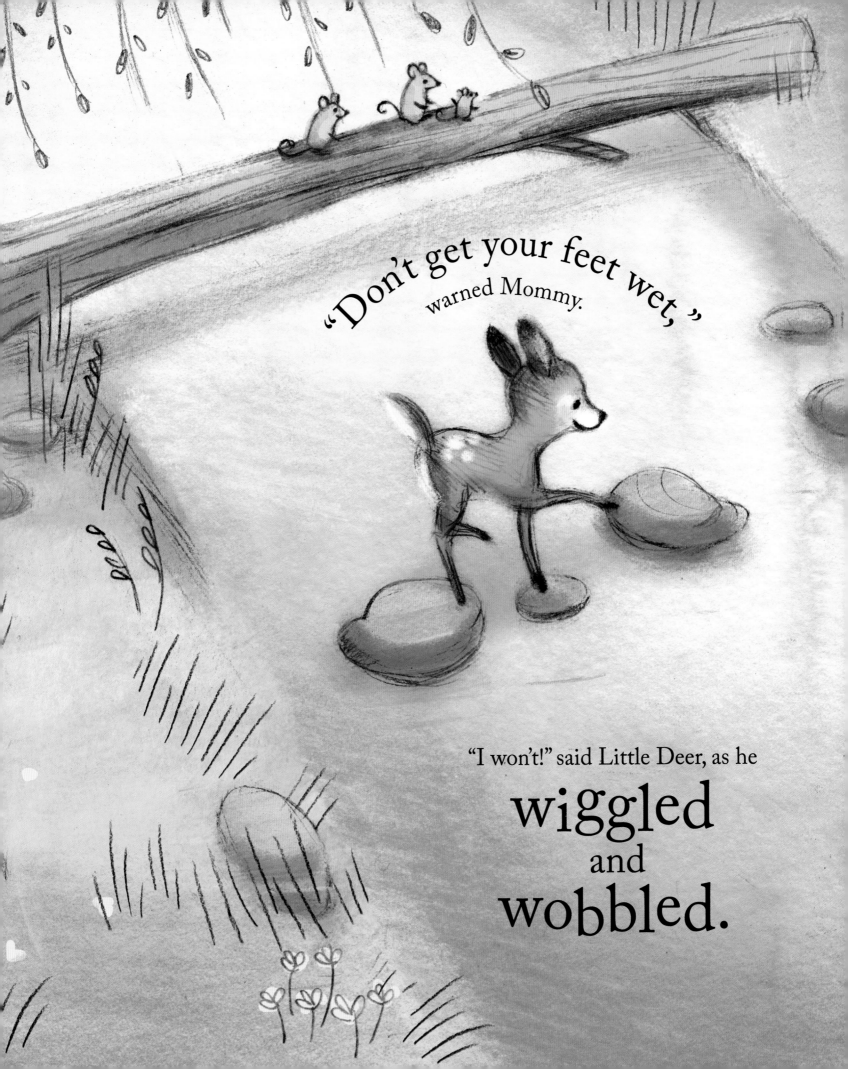

"Don't get your feet wet," warned Mommy.

"I won't!" said Little Deer, as he wiggled and wobbled.

Little Deer counted red and orange butterflies, then squeezed through thick, tangly bushes.

"Don't get stuck," warned Mommy.

"I won't!" called Little Deer, as he skipped out the other side. **"Hurry up, Mommy!"** he called. "There's so much more to see."

"Look!" said Little Deer.
"A hill that goes up to the clouds!"

"Is it too high?" said his mommy.

"It's not too high for me,"

said Little Deer, panting as he climbed step by step all the way to the top.

"I can see **forever!**"
cried Little Deer, standing tall
on his tiptoes.

His mommy stood close beside
him, but Little Deer was
beginning to wobble again,

and suddenly …

"Wheeee!"

cried Little Deer as he
skidded and slid, landing
with a swoosh in a pile of
fallen leaves.

"Are you okay, Little Deer?"
asked his mommy.

"Yes!" giggled Little Deer. "I am!"

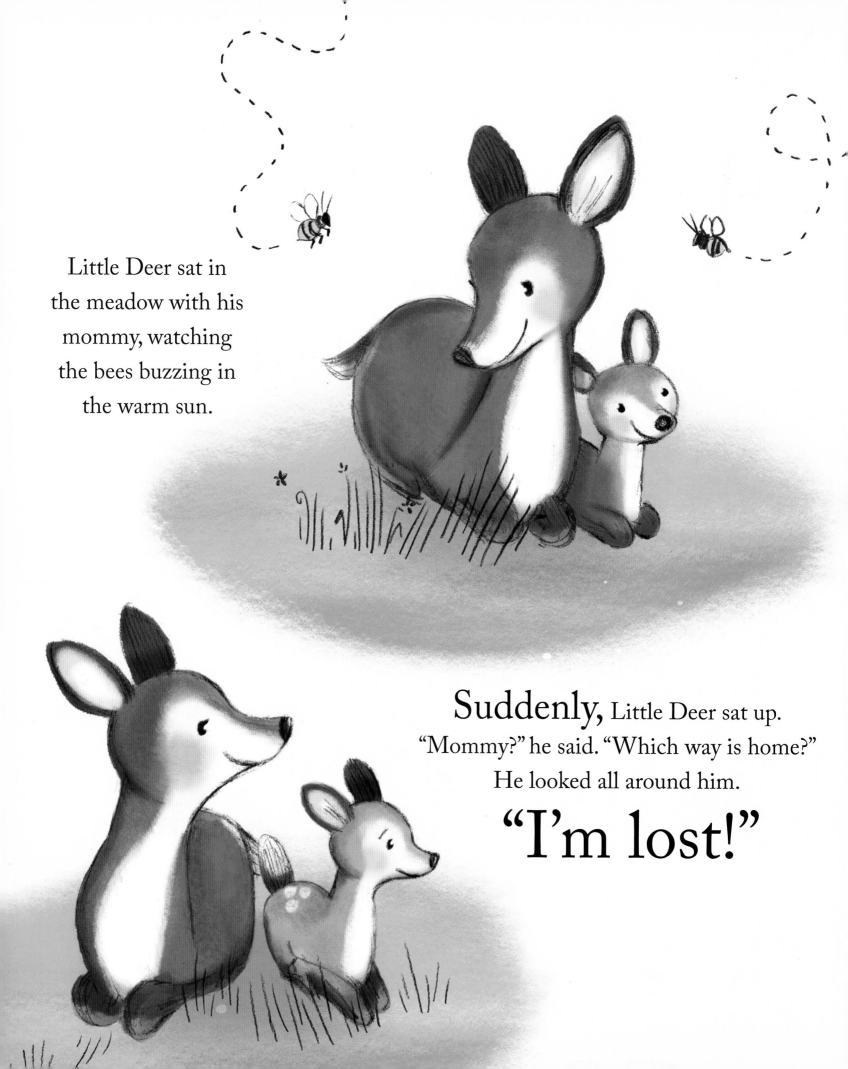

Little Deer sat in the meadow with his mommy, watching the bees buzzing in the warm sun.

Suddenly, Little Deer sat up. "Mommy?" he said. "Which way is home?" He looked all around him.

"I'm lost!"

Mommy Deer nuzzled Little Deer's nose. "We'll soon find our way back," she said soothingly. "We just have to remember how we got here."

Little Deer thought and thought. At last, he began to remember …

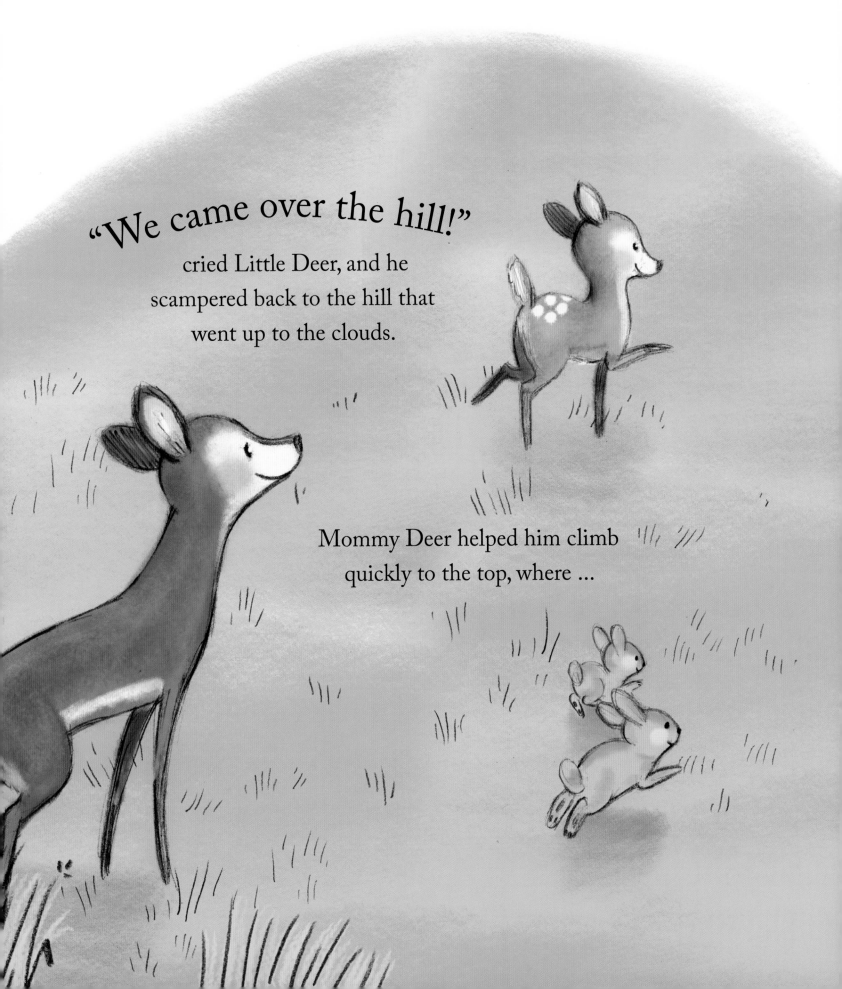

"We came over the hill!"
cried Little Deer, and he
scampered back to the hill that
went up to the clouds.

Mommy Deer helped him climb
quickly to the top, where ...

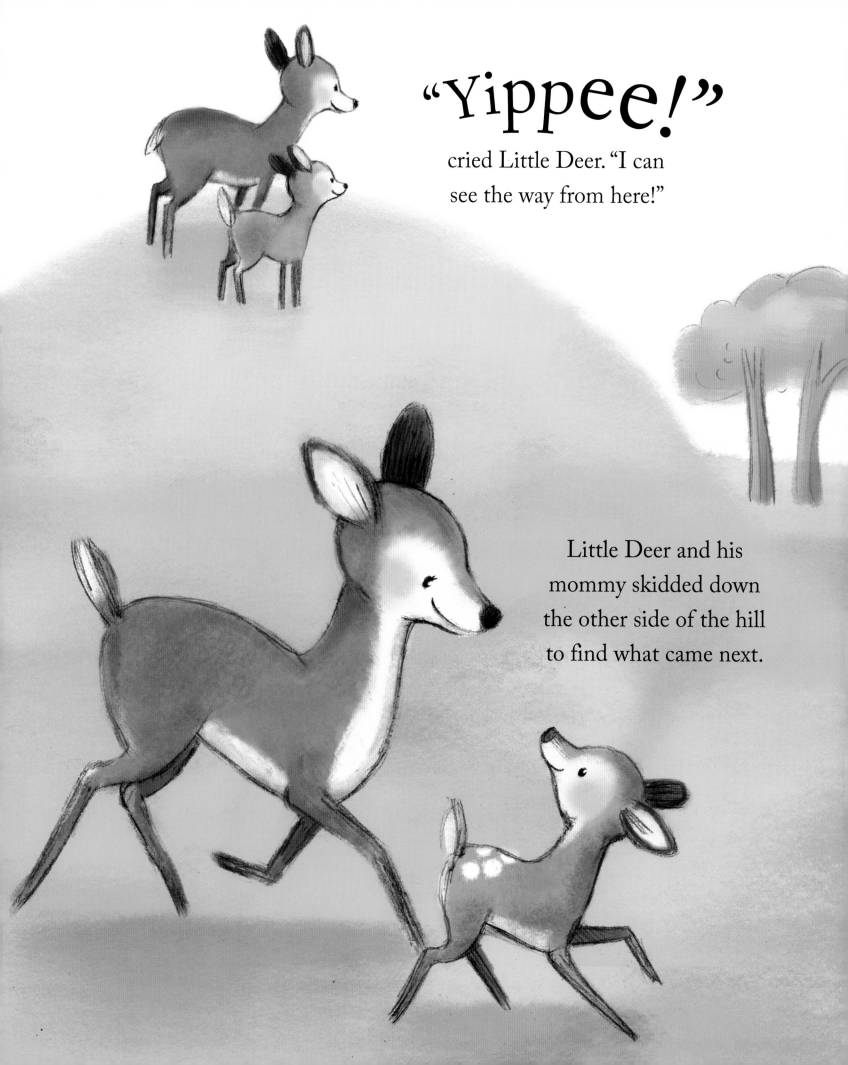

"Yippee!"

cried Little Deer. "I can
see the way from here!"

Little Deer and his
mommy skidded down
the other side of the hill
to find what came next.

"We squeezed through the tangly bushes!" Little
Deer told his mommy, and he scurried back
through the hole he'd made, with his little tail
wagging. Mommy Deer gave him a helping nudge.

"Which way now?" said Little Deer's
mommy, when they were on the other side.
Little Deer saw the red and orange butterflies, and
heard the trickling sound of a stream ...

"The wobbly stones!" cheered
Little Deer, as he hurried across the stream.

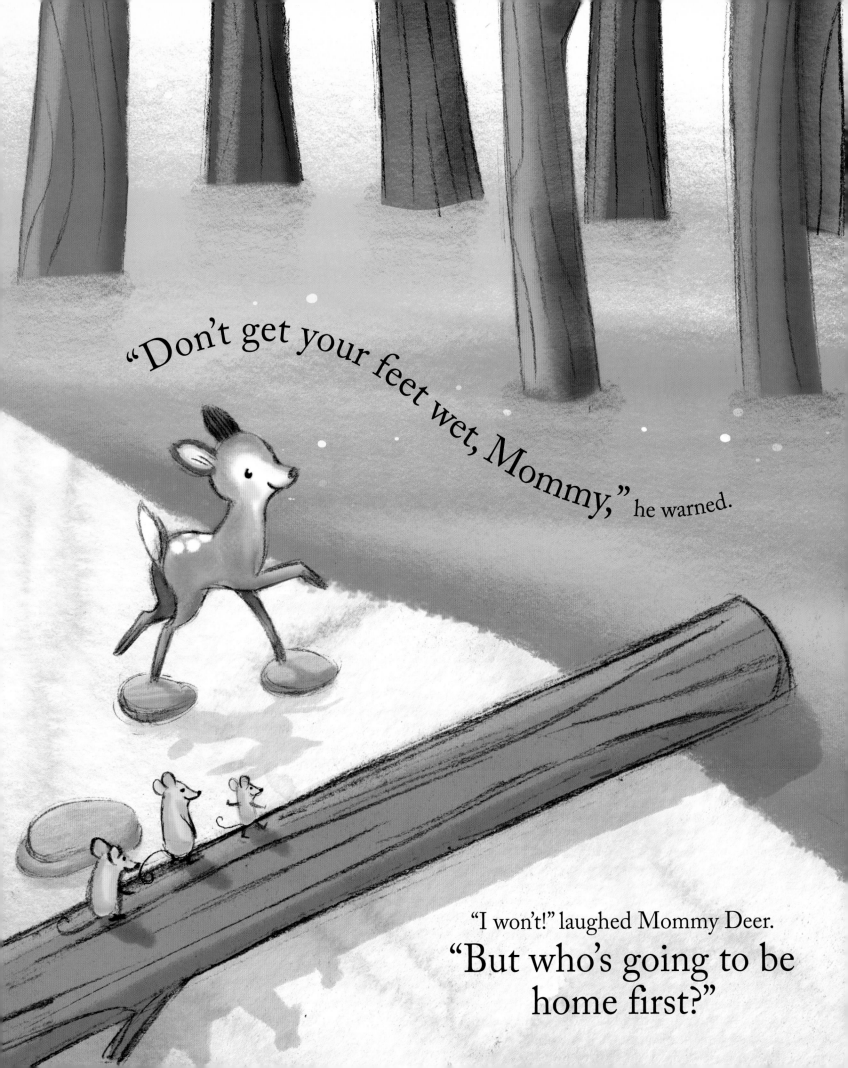

"Don't get your feet wet, Mommy," he warned.

"I won't!" laughed Mommy Deer.
"But who's going to be home first?"

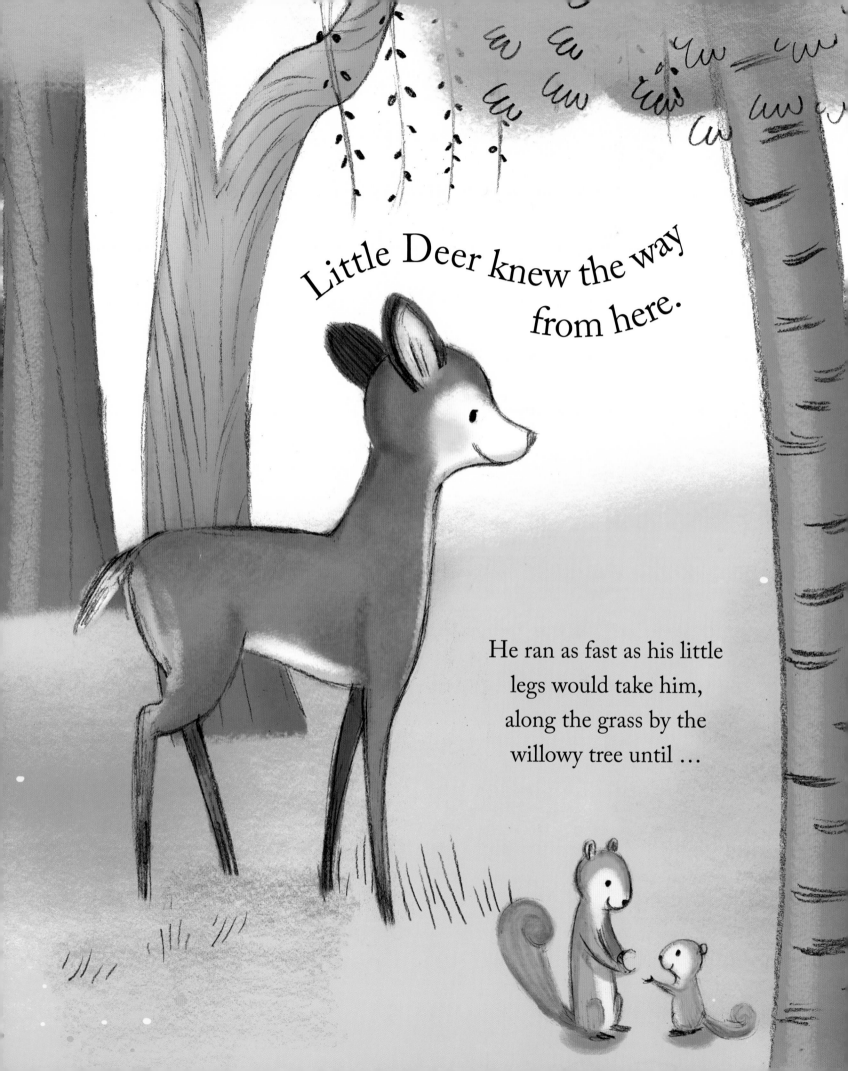

Little Deer knew the way from here.

He ran as fast as his little legs would take him, along the grass by the willowy tree until …

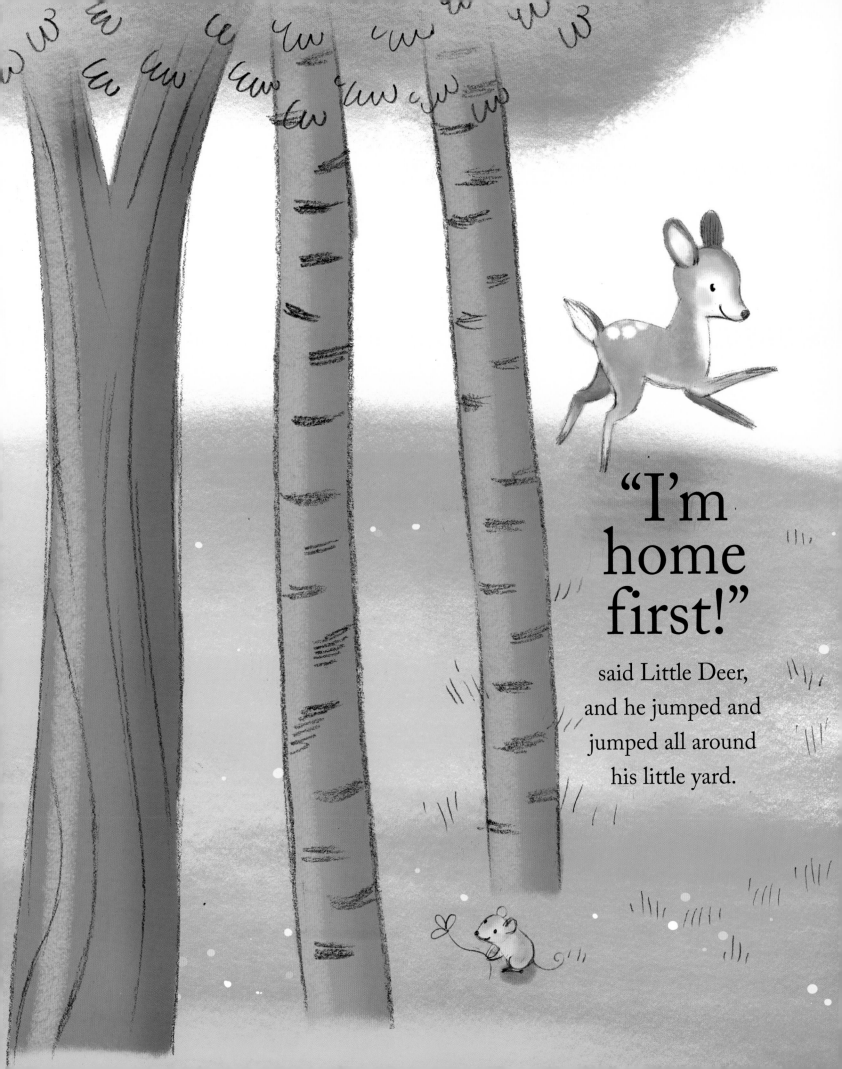

"I'm home first!"

said Little Deer, and he jumped and jumped all around his little yard.

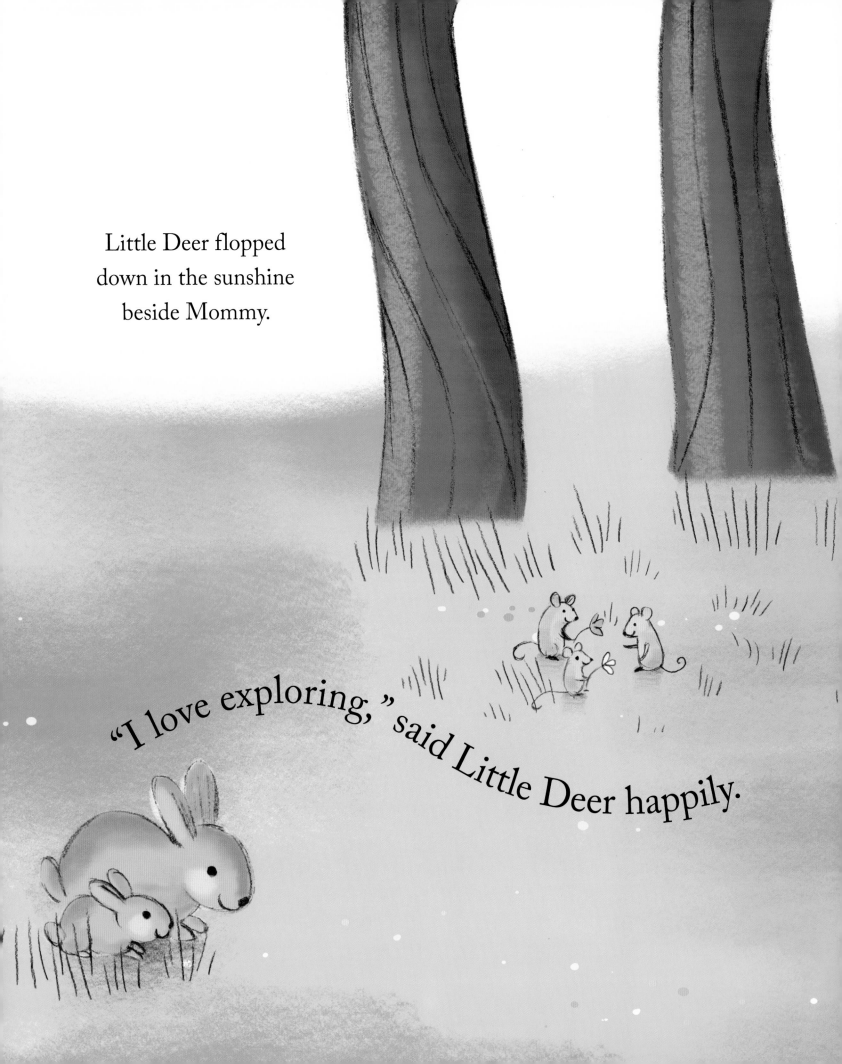

Little Deer flopped
down in the sunshine
beside Mommy.

"I love exploring," said Little Deer happily.

"And I love
my mommy!"